ECHOES OF THE NORTHEAST

A POETIC FOLKLORE AND OTHER POEMS

KRISHNA ACHARYA

Made with ♥ on the Notion Press Platform
www.notionpress.com

From the Author

This book is dedicated to those who have journeyed with me through the landscapes of the heart and the mind. Your presence, encouragement, and love have been the guiding light in my creative process.

To my mother,

Your unwavering support and boundless love have provided the foundation upon which I stand. You have instilled in me the values of hard work, resilience, and the beauty of simplicity. This collection is as much yours as it is mine.

To my siblings, wife and lovely daughter,

You have been my friends and lifelong companions. Your laughter, kindness, and shared memories are woven into the fabric of these poems.

To my friends,

Thank you for being my sounding board, my critics, and my cheerleaders. Your insights, whether gentle or tough, have helped shape my work into what it is today.

To the students and teachers of Navodaya Vidyalaya Samiti,
My beloved workplace, you have been a source of inspiration and joy. The energy, curiosity, and dedication that fill our school have been instrumental in shaping my thoughts and my art. This book is as much a tribute to your spirit as it is a piece of my own heart. Thank you for being part of my journey.

Contents

Contents

Contents

Contents

Contents

Preface

About the Poet

In the tranquil hills of Ri-Bhoi, Meghalaya, amidst the lush greenery, resides Krishna Acharya, a dedicated educator and a passionate poet. By profession, Krishna serves as a Post Graduate Teacher at Jawahar Navodaya Vidyalaya, Ministry of Education, Government of India shaping the minds of the next generation. However, beyond the realms of textbooks and classrooms, Krishna's heart beats to the rhythm of poetry, weaving verses that echo the soul of the Northeast India.

Krishna's poetry intricately intertwines the rich culture, tradition, folklore, and the vibrant personalities that grace the lands of the Northeast. With each stanza, he paints vivid portraits of the region's diversity, capturing the essence of its people, their customs, and the timeless tales that have been passed down through generations.

But Krishna's pen doesn't merely dwell on the tangible; it also traverses the landscapes of imagination, exploring the unseen realms of emotion and spirituality. Through his verses, he invites readers on a journey to discover the hidden gems of Northeast India, from the serene landscapes to the bustling markets, from the ancient rituals to the modern aspirations.

Beyond his literary pursuits, Krishna finds solace and joy in the simple pleasures of life. Whether it's imparting knowledge to eager minds in the classroom, honing his skills on the cricket field, or engaging in heartfelt conversations with strangers turned friends, Krishna embodies the spirit of curiosity and connection.

As an aspiring writer and poet, Krishna Acharya's debut collection is a testament to his love for his homeland and his unwavering commitment to sharing its beauty with the world. Through his words, he invites readers to immerse themselves in the enchanting life of Northeast India, where every verse is a celebration of life, love, and the enduring spirit of its people.

You can get in touch with Krishna via:

Facebook: https://www.facebook.com/profile.php?id=100005425451754

Email: acharya.jnv@gmail.com

About the Book

Echoes of the Northeast is a captivating collection that weaves together the essence of Northeast Indian culture, food, folklore, and tribal lives through the medium of poetry. Each poem in this anthology serves as a lyrical exploration, delving into the rich tapestry of traditions, beliefs, and customs that characterize the region. From Sattriya of Assam to the mystical tales of Nagaland, the verses transport readers on a journey through the vibrant landscapes and diverse communities of Northeast India and the Darjeeling Hills.

Through the poet's evocative language, readers are immersed in the sights, sounds, and flavors of the region, as well as the timeless stories passed down through generations. The collection also pays homage to the renowned personalities who have left an indelible mark on Northeast Indian history and culture, celebrating their contributions and legacies. In addition, the poet also expresses his other powerful emotions in other poems that compel the readers to think and introspect.

Echoes of the Northeast is not just a literary work but a celebration of the spirit and resilience of the people who call this region home. It invites readers to ponder the beauty of tradition, the complexity of identity, and the interconnectedness of humanity, all through the lens of a poetic expression.

Acknowledgements

Writing Echoes of the Northeast has been a journey filled with invaluable support and encouragement from individuals who have greatly impacted my work. I would like to express my deepest gratitude to my brother, Govinda Acharya, for his all-round assistance; his unwavering support has been a foundation throughout this endeavor. I am also immensely grateful to Dr. Sandeep Tiwary and Mr. Jai Kishan Jillowa of Kendriya Vidyalaya NEPA Barapani, whose guidance has been instrumental to this project. Special thanks to Mr. Nirmal Bhattarai of Ri- Bhoi, Meghalaya and Mr. Sashi Rai of Jawahar Navodaya Vidyalaya, Gomati, for their encouragement and motivation at every step. I extend my gratitude to Motivational Stripes family for pushing me to where I am today in my poetic journey.

I extend my heartfelt thanks to my dear friend Dr. Arjun Chetry, Assistant Director (IT) at Northeastern Police Academy, for his relentless inspiration to push beyond limits and strive for excellence. His constant motivation to go that extra mile has been a driving force behind this work.

To each of you, thank you for helping to make this book a reality.

Table Of Contents

1. Banjkahri

In the depths of forests where they dance,
Where mystic whispers weave a trance,
There dwells a duo, ancient and wild,
Banjhakri and Banjhakrini, untamed and beguiled.
Banjhakri, the trickster with ears so large,
A forested shaman, an enigmatic charge,
Sun's descendant, with matted hair and golden drum,
Guiding chosen ones where the spirits hum.
Banjhakrini, ursine and humanoid in her form,
Bloodthirsty yet nurturing, in the forest storm,
Long hair cascades, backward feet leave prints unseen,
In her embrace, a shaman's fate begins, serene.
Legends tell of their abductions, both feared and revered,
Children chosen, into their realm steered,
In caverns deep, where initiation breathes,
Shamanic secrets whisper through ancient leaves.
They walk between worlds, seen by the chosen few,
Guardians of nature, their presence true,
In Darjeeling hills and Sikkim's terrace,
Their essence lingers, mystic and grace.
Banjhakri and Banjhakrini, spirits wise,
Teaching wisdom from the time rise,
In forests deep, where they roam free,
They shape destiny with shamanic decree.

So listen closely to the forest's call,
Where Banjhakri's drum beats, summoning all,
And Banjhakrini's gaze, fierce yet kind,
Guides the chosen to realms undefined.
In the heart of nature, Banjhakri reside,
And Banjhakrini on his side,
Shamans, guardians of the forests,
Trains and teaches the little guests.

2. Sorah Shraddh

In the golden light of Bhadra's morn,
Where whispers of ancestors are reborn,
We gather by rivers, calm and wide,
To observe Sorah Shradh in the open tide.
Sixteenth day, a solemn rite,
Underneath the sun's gentle light,
We offer prayers with reverence deep,
For those in the family in eternal sleep.
Rice and lentils, offerings made,
To honour ancestors' guiding shade,
Their blessings sought, with holy spirits near,
In this sacred time of the year.
With folded hands and voices clear,
Mantras echo for all to hear,
Each gesture, each hymn, a heartfelt plea,
For grace and blessings, pure and free.
Sorah Sradha, a sacred start,
To Dashain's joy, where spirits impart,
Strength and love from ages past,
This lovely bond forever last.
In the golden light of Bhadra's morn,
Where whispers of ancestors are reborn,
Sorah Sradha's connect we stand,
Guided by their eternal hand.

3. Langsimbruid

In Jaintia's hills' ringing of morning bell,
Amidst green slopes where legends dwell,
A sport of strength, of bulls untamed,
Langsimbruid, where honour claimed.
In winter mornings, drums resound,
As villagers gather all around,
With hearts that beat in rhythmic cheer,
To witness bulls with courage sheer.
Amidst the fields, the bulls engage,
In ancient ritual, proud on stage,
Hooves thunder, mighty horns clash,
Langsimbruid shows the energetic flash.
From distant valleys, tribes convene,
In Langsimbruid, a sacred scene,
Where lineage and pride shine,
In battles fierce, holding the chilling spine.
For each stride marks a tale untold,
Of courage, valor, legends bold,
In Jaintia's hills, this sport endures,
Langsimbruid, where tradition secures.
So raise the banner, let the drums beat,
In Langsimbruid, where clans compete,
For honour, glory, and ancestral pride,
In timeless bonds that never subside.

4. Sakewa

With 'doko' and 'namlo' a culture deep,
Kirati life, not so cheap.
Grounded in nature, with hearts clear,
Sakewa's rhythm, a festive to cheer
Ubhauli's promise, a fertile land
Sowing done with dexterous hand.
In walk up the hill, a melody heard,
Of a beautiful golden robin bird.
Udhauli's gives a plenty harvest,
Yuma's blessings and his grace.
A kirati stand solid and tall.
They stand proud and never fall
From their culture and rural life creed,A
The most lovely people of Himalayan breed

5. Lonely Retiree

A life well-lived, yet now feels overthrown with memories deep,
He gave his all, but now he's left to weep.
From dawn to dusk, he labored, gave his best,
Sacrificing dreams for family's behest.
His children, now successful, far away,
In foreign lands, their lives in bright array.
His wife, a constant partner in the past,
Now with their kids, her presence did not last.
A house once filled with laughter, now a shell,
His heart, once full, now echoes like a bell.
He looks back on the years with quiet sighs,
The moments missed, the tears within his eyes.
He wonders, did his love go all in vain?
A lifetime spent, now met with silent pain.
High blood pressure and ailments of the old,
A body tired, a spirit growing cold.
Yet in his heart, a flicker of a dream,
That life could be more balanced than it seems.
He yearns for calls, a touch, a warm embrace,
But days go by, he sees no friendly face.
The sacrifice he made, the love he gave,
Seem distant now, like waves upon the grave.
Yet hope remains, a spark within the night,
For men like him, still searching for the light.

To love themselves, to find a way to cope,
To build a life that's filled with more than hope.
So here's to men who gave their all away,
May they find peace and joy along the way.
To cherish self, to live, to truly see,
Their worth, their love, their legacy.

6. Northeast's Gateway-Coronation Bridge

Across the Teesta's rushing tide,
Coronation Bridge, in steel does confide.
A king's decree, a bygone age,
Yet, purpose strong, upon this stage.
Truss and arch, a structure grand,
Defying currents, on shifting sand.
A marvel wrought, in years of yore,
Connecting lands, forevermore.
From Darjeeling's slopes, to Kalimpong's green,
A vital thread, a vibrant scene.
Northeast's gateway, to the nation wide,
On National Highway, with steady stride.
Below, the river, whispers heard,
Unheard stories in old man's word.
A fleeting glimpse, for travelers' eyes,
A scenic canvas, painted in the skies.
More than steel, a symbol stands,
Of human will, on shifting sands.
Through floods and quakes, it holds its ground,
A testament to progress, all around.
So let the Coronation Bridge remain,
A silent witness, to sun and rain.

A mark of history, etched in time,
A bridge of steel, with purpose sublime.

7. 7 Sisters Hand in Hand

Seven sisters, hand in hand,
Daughters of the eastern land.
From Assam's plains, where Brahma flows,
To Arunachal's peaks, where winter snows.
Meghalaya's mist, on flourishing hills,
Manipur's jewels, with dancing skills.
Mizoram's bamboo forests sing,
Nagaland's warriors, freedom bring.
Tripura's lakes, a tranquil dream,
Sikkim's monasteries, sunlight's gleam.
Diverse in customs, rich and bold,
An interwoven, stories told.
From Khasi whispers, soft and low,
To Mizo melodies, that sweetly flow.
Bihu's rhythm, Hornbill's flight,
Festivals vibrant, bathed in light.
Spicy curries, with a citrus zest,
Silk handlooms, the finest dress.
Headhunters' tales, and weaving art,
A land that captures every heart.
Strong and independent, spirits high,
The seven sisters, reaching for the sky.
Unity in difference, their voices blend,
A Northeast symphony, that knows no end.

8. In the Land of the Rising Sun

In the land of rising sun, where Himalayan topline,
Arunachal Pradesh, a cultural shrine.
Twenty-six tribes strong, their voices ring so true,
Each with traditions, whispers of the old and new.
Donyi-Polo's wisdom, is heard in the air,
Sun and moon as deities, guiding everywhere.
Harmony sought, with every living thing,
A reverence for forests, where spirits take wing.
Skilled hands weave magic, on looms so bright,
Carpets, paintings, woodcarvings, a dazzling sight.
Bamboo whispers secrets, in baskets crafted fine,
Art forms passed down, a heritage that will shine.
Festivals erupt, with color, song, and dance,
Losar's joy, Solung's strength, a joyous trance.
Aji Lamu's grace, Chalo's playful beat,
Nokte's martial spirit, tapping rhythmic feet.
Languages so many, a symphony untold,
Tibeto-Burman whispers, stories yet unfold.
Nyishi, Apatani, echoes on the breeze,
Mishmi in the east, whispering through the trees.
From arranged unions, to elopement's call,
Wedding rituals, blessings upon all.

Yellow chains of bamboo, a bond that will hold,
Sugar's sweet welcome, a story to be told.
Ancient beliefs linger, in every tribe's heart,
Spirits benevolent, playing a sacred part.
The Dandai's wisdom, dispelling every fear,
Sacrifices offered, for a future crystal clear.

9. Deusi Bhailo and a Nimble Feet

In every heart a Tihar's lights ignite,
Deusi Bhailo dances, decorate diwali night.
Men and women, in joyous throng,
Sing and step, where music belong.
Deusi's call, on a madal's beat,
Bhailo's grace, with nimble feet.
Flutes and dholki, a rhythmic sound,
Echoing blessings, all around.
House to house, deusi team goes,
Songs of harvest, story shows,
Blessings offered, for wealth and cheer,
As the New Year's promise draws near.
Dakshina's gifts, a sweet reward,
For melodies shared and for every word.
Colorful dresses, with vibrant shade,
Reflecting culture, that time embed.
Ancestral tradition, warmly held,
In every step, a story spelled.
Community strong, spirits high,
Deusi Bhailo, reaching for the sky.
Tihar's flame, a guiding light,
Deusi Bhailo, dancing through the night.

Lovely beats in every rhyme,
A cultural treasure, for all of time.

10. Sorathi and Madal

In Himalayan air, where Robin birds fly,
Nepali Sorathi, a joyous cry.
Lively rhythm, on madal's beat,
A call and response, voices meet.
From Sikkim's slopes, to Darjeeling's grace,
Sorathi's melody, sets the heart apace.
Flutes like whispers, and dholki's call,
Stories of old, for one and all.
Love's sweet yearning, in a maiden's song,
Of harvest bounty, where fields grow strong.
Social commentary, with wit so keen,
Life's story, on a vigorous scene.
Dashain's bright lights, Tihar's festive cheer,
Sorathi echoes, ringing near.
Ancient tales, of heroes bold,
In songs they live, never to grow old.
Nepali spirit, in every note,
Sorathi's magic with wonderful quote.
A bridge between past, present, and dreams,
A cultural treasure, forever it seems.
So let the Sorathi, forever ring,
In Kanchenjunga foothills, where Nepalis sing.
A song of community, joy, and pride,
Nepali Sorathi, for eternity will reside.

11. Risa Weaves Tales of the Tradition

In Tipraland, where looms click and clack,
A woven wonder, on weavers' back.
Risa, the cloth, a creamy delight,
Handcrafted beauty, bathed in sunlight.
Tripuri women, with practiced hand,
Weave tales of tradition, across the land.
Reang and Jamatia, Noatia too,
Their threads interlock, sparkling and true.
Cotton so soft, or silken sheen,
Risa's embrace comforting the teen.
Borders of magic, in colors so bright,
Geometric patterns, a geometric delight.
Wrapped with grace, a woman's attire,
Or a heady scarf, setting hearts afire.
For carrying babes, a cradle so sweet,
Risa's embrace, can't be beat.
A cultural treasure, a tradition grand,
Passed down through generations, hand in hand.
Each thread a whisper, a story unfold,
Of Tripura's spirit, brave and bold.
So let Risa flourish, with every design,
A symbol of unity, forever to shine.

A woven testament of tribes strong and free,
Risa's magic wraps you, for eternity.

12. Fiery Leader Bhagwan Birsa Munda

In Munda's home, where strength reside,
Bhagwan Birsa Munda, with courage as his guide.
A fiery leader, with freedom's call,
For Adivasi rights, he stood tall.
Against land grabbers, and taxes unjust,
His voice rose strong, a flicker of trust.
"Abua Desh, Abua Raj!" he cried,
Our land, our rule, let freedom abide!
He preached renewal, a faith reborn,
Hare Gomke's message, against societal scorn.
Equality sought, for all to see,
Unity forged, under a Sal tree.
The British might, he dared to defy,
Guerilla tactics, beneath a fiery sky.
Though flames were doused, his bravery inspires,
A legacy burning, with righteous fires.
(Hare Gomke is a title or phrase used within the Munda religion or culture to signify a spiritual leader.)

13. A Legend of Marang Buru

In the tea gardens the spirits roam,
A legend whispers, of Marang Buru's home.
The great one, the first, the all-knowing hand,
Who shaped the world, across the sand.

From the gusty winds and starlit night,
Marang Buru spoke, with radiant light.
Mountains rose, at his command,
Rivers flowed, across the land.

Trees whistling, in a graceful dress,
Animals roamed, with nature's bless.
Sun and moon, he set their course,
Guiding day and night, a constant force.

But darkness lurked, in shadows deep,
Malevolent spirits, secrets to keep.
Marang Buru fought, with thunder's roar,
Banishing evil and violent snore.

Then from the earth, a precious spark,
He breathed life's essence, left its mark.

The first Santhal, with hopeful eyes,
A bond with nature under blue skies.

Marang Buru watches with watchful eyes,
Guiding their steps keeping fear aside
In festivals big the offerings made,
The Santhals honor, the light that pervaded.

So echoes the legend, from hearts devout,
Marang Buru's presence, filling them throughout.
The Santhali moves and 'Sereng' they sung,
The hardworking clan to which they belong.

14. Hahasa and Dishimoni- A Santhal Folklore

In the world unseen, where beautiful souls played,
A bamboo grove in the sunlight swayed.
From its green stalks, a folklore grew,
Two souls emerged, bathed in morning dew.
Pilchu Haram, the sacred grove,
Birthed the first Santhal, a story of love.
Hahasa, the man, with strength and grace,
Dishimoni, the woman, with beauty's embrace.
Hand in hand, they stepped into light,
The world unfolded, vast and bright.
Stars as their guide, on moonlit trails,
Learning nature's songs, and whispering gales.
The language of birds, the secrets of trees,
The whispers of wind, carried on the breeze.
Pilchu Haram's magic, forever their own,
Guiding their steps, a place to call home.
From this sacred birth, a lineage began,
The Santhal people, across the land.
Honoring Pilchu Haram, with grateful sigh,
Where life first came down the mountains high.
So echoes the myth, in voice of nature,
The Santhal spirit existed altogether.

A bond with forests, forever made,
Pilchu Haram's folklore will never fade.
In the world unseen, where beautiful souls played,
A bamboo grove in the sunlight swayed.
From its green stalks, a folklore grew,
Two souls emerged, bathed in morning dew.

Pilchu Haram, the sacred grove,
Birthed the first Santhal, a story of love.
Hahasa, the man, with strength and grace,
Dishimoni, the woman, with beauty's embrace.

Hand in hand, they stepped into light,
The world unfolded, vast and bright.
Stars as their guide, on moonlit trails,
Learning nature's songs, and whispering gales.
The language of birds, the secrets of trees,
The whispers of wind, carried on the breeze.
Pilchu Haram's magic, forever their own,
Guiding their steps, a place to call home.
From this sacred birth, a lineage began,
The Santhal people, across the land.
Honoring Pilchu Haram, with grateful sigh,
Where life first came down the mountains high.
So echoes the myth, in voice of nature,
The Santhal spirit existed altogether.
A bond with forests, forever made,
Pilchu Haram's folklore will never fade.

15. Santhali Folklore: The Hare and the Moon

In tea gardens, Santhali stories bloom,
A fable whispers, dispelling gloom.
The Hare and Moon, a tale unfolds,
Of cunning plans and truths untold.
The Hare, known quick, with fur like snow,
Met a hungry Tiger, rumbling low.
The Tiger growled, with eyes aflame,
"Tonight you dine, a tasty game!"
The Hare, unfazed, with wit so keen,
Spied a firefly's flickering sheen.
"Greater prey awaits," he said,
"A celestial beast, overhead!"
He led the Tiger, through moonlit night,
To a shimmering well, a wondrous sight.
"The Moon Beast dwells," the Hare declared,
"His reflection, in this water shared!"
The Tiger peered, with stripes ablaze,
Saw his own form, in the moonlit haze.
Leaping high, with fearsome roar,
He plunged into the well's cool core.
The Hare watched, then chuckled low,
The Tiger's hunger, met a watery woe.

But from the Moon, a voice did boom,
"Deception's price, will fill your room!"
The Hare's fur, once pure and white,
Turned spotted grey, beneath the night.
A constant mark, for all to see,
Honesty's path, sets you truly free.
So whispers the tale, from ages old,
In Santhal lands, a truth unfolds.
Let cunning ways, and lies depart,
For honesty's light, will guide your heart.

16. Hajong Women Unique and Bright

In plains of Axom where silk gleam,
Hajong women, the female supreme.
Patini's swirl, a rainbow bright,
Woven tales in fabric's light.
Skilled hands weave, with practiced grace,
Threads of joy on nature's face.
Yellow, green, and crimson bold,
A story whispered, here it unfold.
From cane and bamboo, thin and tall,
They craft creations, big and small.
Baskets woven, sturdy and neat,
Holding treasures, garden's sweet.
More than beauty, their spirit gleams,
Resilience woven in their dreams.
Hajong women, bold and bright,
Culture's flame, a blazing light.

17. Karbi Culture Bright and True

In the place where Kopili flow,
Karbi society, a structure aglow.
Patriarchal roots, a lineage strong,
Clans and sub-clans, where they belong.
Five Kur stand tall, handsome and bright,
Terang, Teron, Enghee, Timung's stride,
Engti completes, a circle whole,
Each with Millim, a branched out soul.
Hendam binds close, families near,
Exogamy's rule, tradition clear.
Marriages arranged, with careful hand,
Harmony all over the Karbi land.
Lindok leads wise, with elders' decree,
Guiding the village, for all to see.
But change whispers soft, on modern breeze,
Education's touch, and shifting seas.
Yet, the core remains, a structure brand,
A Karbi tribe gentle at hand.
From ancient roots, to branches new,
Karbi culture is unique and true.

18. Hen- The Industrious Queen; A Karbi Folklore

In a coop by the rice paddies so green,
Lived a Hen, a most industrious queen.
From sunrise to dusk, she'd work with such care,
While her friends lazed about, with nary a share.
The Dog loved his naps, the Cat chased butterflies bright,
The bookwormish Mouse, lost in stories of night.
The Hen, with a sigh, cleaned, gathered, and fed,
Wishing her friends would lend her a tread.
One day, tired and worn, with a devious glint,
The Hen chose to rest, not a single chore to stint.
The coop fell in disarray, a cluttered domain,
As the friends woke to their folly and pain.
The Dog with no bed, the Cat with no hay,
The Mouse with no breakfast, not a single stray seed they could say.
Shamefaced they came, with apologies true,
"Please help us, dear Hen, we'll see this chore through!"
From then on, they worked, a coop spick and span,
A lesson well learnt, for every woman and man.
Together they thrived, a coop strong,
Cooperation is the key, a moral lesson learnt.

19. Sirwomu Praise

In Karbi Anglong, where hills connect,
A legend whispers wrecked unwrecked.
Sirwomu's tale, on voices fly,
Of a hunter's courage, down the blue sky.
Two monstrous birds, with wings of dread,
The Womu called, a haunting spread.
They stole the crops, and cast a blight,
Fear filled the days, and darkened night.
But Sirwomu rose, with heart aflame,
A sharpened spear, to end the game.
He tracked their nests, in mountains high,
A perilous climb, under the sky.
With steady hand, and piercing gaze,
He faced the Womu, in a fiery maze.
The battle raged, with feathers strewn,
The earth did tremble, beneath the moon.
Sirwomu fought, with strength and might,
His arrows sharp, a piercing light.
The Womu fell, with deafening cries,
And freedom bloomed, in the Karbi skies.
From then on, songs Sirwomu praise,
The hunter brave, in olden days.
A symbol strong, for all to see,
Of valour and fearless victory.

20. Umngot River a Serene Embrace

Crystal clear as the sky's own hue,
Umngot river, a mirror true.
Down the hills, its waters flow,
Reflecting the world with a gentle glow.
Divers plunge, with hearts elate,
Into waters pure, where dreams await.
In every dive, a moment to savor,
In Umngot's embrace, joy finds its flavor.
In the depths, a world unseen,
Where silence reigns, and peace convenes.
Umngot's whispers, soft and clear,
Echo through time, drawing hearts near.
As clear as the sky, this river divine,
Where fish glide, and pearls brightly shine.
In Umngot's depths, pebbles dance with glee,
Visible treasures for all to see.
Just a stone's throw from Shillong's grace,
Umngot flows, a serene embrace
Where dreams arise and hearts tend,
In the river's depth, time seem to bend.

21. Kwai

In the abode of clouds and mountain's crest,
Where Khasi hearts beat strong and blessed,
A tradition cherished, time-honored and true,
In every home, in every view.
In every hearth, with warmth and zest,
Betel nut and leaf, by love confessed,
A symbol of kinship, in hues so bright,
Welcoming guests from dawn till night.
With reverence and respect, they're bestowed,
A gift of honor, a debt that's owed,
In Khasi homes, where hearts are kind,
Betel nut and leaf, forever bind.
With each chew, a bond is formed,
A bridge of friendship, through time adorned,
Conversation flows, like rivers wide,
As laughter echoes, side by side.
In Khasi tradition, this ritual sublime,
Echoes the spirit of a bygone time,
Where hospitality reigns supreme,
And betel nut and leaf fulfill the dream.
So let us raise a toast, to this cherished art,
That binds us close, and warms the heart,
In the land of Khasi, where clouds roam,
Kwai pathi and shun, find its home.

22. In Sumer Village Where Life's a Song

In Sumer's village, where life's a dance,
'Midst hills and streams, where dreams enhance,
The school stands tall shining bright,
Amidst the day and evening's light.
Beside the school, the MRF's beat,
Retreading tyres in rhythm's feat,
While Kala Bazar paints hues so fine,
In Sumer's tale, its colors shine.
And o'er the fields, the playground calls,
Where footballers chase and spirits sprawl,
With every kick, a dream takes flight,
In Sumer's tale, beneath the light.
At dawn's first blush, the joggers tread,
In morning's hush, their paths they spread,
A rhythm set by steps so sure,
In Sumer's tale, their hearts allure.
As day gives way to evening's glow,
Fast food aromas gently flow,
And joggers pause, and footballers rest,
In Sumer's tale, they find their nest.
And when the stars adorn the sky,
With pegs of wine, the spirits fly,

In Sumer's village, where life's a song,
Amidst the day, the night, so long.

23. Their Love Endures Forevermore

In the halls of college, love did bloom,
Two souls entwined, their hearts in tune.
Through laughter and tears, they forged their way,
In the golden light of a youthful day.
Hand in hand, they walked the miles,
Sharing dreams and secret smiles.
But shadows fell upon their bliss,
A rift emerged, a lover's abyss.
Misunderstanding cast its darkened veil,
And love's sweet song began to pale.
They parted ways, their hearts adrift,
In the ebb and flow of a painful rift.
She found solace in another's embrace,
While he delved deep into words, finding grace.
In the ink-stained nights, he poured his soul,
Turning heartache into stories untold.

Years passed by, and fame embraced his name,
Yet echoes of her lingered in his flame.
She, too, found him in the pages turned,
His love and loss, the lessons learned.
As fate's gentle hand led them to meet,

Old wounds reopened, hearts skipped a beat.
In the quiet of reunion's embrace,
They found forgiveness, a sacred space.
Though their love's journey reached its close,
Its echoes lingered, like a fragrant rose.
In the walls of their intertwined fate,
Their story endures, a timeless state.

For love, though fleeting, leaves its mark,
In the depths of souls, in the lightest spark.
And though they walked separate shores,
Their love endures, more and more.

24. Huyen Lallong

In the land where hills hold secrets deep,
Where echoes dance and whispers creep,
Huiyen Lallong, a tale to keep,
In martial grace, its warriors leap.
From the land of gems heart, it did arise,
Beneath vast skies and watchful eyes,
Fluid forms beneath the sun's disguise,
In every step, a legacy lies.
With Thang that sing and Ta that soar,
They weave their tales, their lore restore,
Through artistry, they seek to explore,
The essence of battles fought before.
In Huiyen's dance, a rhythm flows,
Each motion tells of ancient throes,
With every strike, a story grows,
Of valor, honor, and warrior's woes.
So let us cherish this art profound,
With each movement, its spirit's found,
In Huiyen's grace, a world unbound,
Where past and present become one sound.

25. Loktak Lake in the Land of Gems

In the land of gems, Loktak Lake lies still,
Reflections of beauty, where dreams fulfill.
Woven with Phumdis, floating isles so rare,
Nature's canvas is beyond compare.
Lotus blooms dance on waters serene,
Whispering folklore of lands unseen.
Fishermen's boats glide, a timeless glide,
In harmony with the lake's gentle stride.
Birds in flight, a symphony above,
Serenading the lake, with songs of love.
O Loktak! Jewel of Manipur's grace,
A sanctuary where culture embrace.
In every ripple, a story untold,
In every breeze, a legend unfold.
Loktak Lake, a treasure to cherish,
In its embrace, all souls flourish.

26. Echoes of the Past

In the sepia tones of yesteryears' embrace,
Old photographs unveil a tender space.
A glimpse of love, once fervently shared,
Now captured in moments, fragile and bared.
Faces etched with smiles, eyes gleaming bright,
Each frame whispers tales of a shared delight.
Hand in hand, amidst life's winding maze,
Two souls danced through the sunlit days.
But time, relentless, weaves its silent thread,
And parted ways, the path diverged and spread.
Yet in the album's pages, memories reside,
A testament to love that once fiercely defied.
Through faded hues and memories' haze,
The heart finds solace in these bygone days.
For though we've journeyed on, paths apart,
In these old pictures, love remains an art.
So let us cherish these echoes of the past,
Each snapshot a reminder, meant to last.
For in the tapestry of time, though we may roam,
The love we shared forever finds a home.

27. Swatantra Senani Shaheed Major Durga Malla

In the hills of Dehradun, where the Gorkhas proudly stand,
Lies the tale of Major Durga Malla, a hero of the land.
Born into Thakuri lineage, his heart ablaze with fire,
He marched with Gandhi's vision, against the British empire.
From student to soldier, his path was clear and bold,
In the ranks of the Gorkha Rifles, his courage we behold.
Joining the INA, with Netaji Bose's call,
He rose to the rank of Major, ready to give his all.
In the shadows of Kohima, where battles fierce were fought,
Malla stood with honor, his every action sought.
Captured by the enemy, his fate sealed by their decree,
Yet he faced his trial with dignity, his spirit ever free.
"The sacrifice I offer shall not be in vain,
India will be free," he said, amidst sorrow and pain.
To his beloved Sharda, his words of strength he gave,
As he stood for his convictions, steadfast and brave.
Married in the shadow of uncertainty, his love never waned,
Even as the gallows awaited, his spirit remained unchained.
On Martyrs' Day we remember, his sacrifice so grand,
Major Durga Malla, forever etched in our land.
With statues raised in honor, his memory we uphold,
A symbol of courage and sacrifice, courageous and bold.

In the heart of every Gorkha, his legacy shall stay,
Major Durga Malla, guiding us on our way.

28. Brave Warrior Captain K. C. Nongrum

Amidst the peaks of Kargil, where the echoes of war resound,
Lies the tale of a hero, with courage truly profound.
Captain K.C. Nongrum, in the Army he did stand,
Brave, strong and resolute, defending the motherland.
In the hour of conflict, where valour meets the foe,
He bore the weight of duty, he had task to do.
In the summer of '99, when the mountains echoed strife,
He fought for his nation and sacrificed his life.
Through piercing bullets, and the thunder of fight,
He stood as a guardian, with all his might.
But in the heat of battle, where heroes are made,
He made the ultimate sacrifice, painted the soil red.
For his bravery in battle, and his valour on that hill,
Captain K.C. Nongrum, we honor you still.
In the chronicle of history, your name will shine bright,
A gallantry of courage, in the darkest of night.
Rest in peace, brave warrior, in your eternal bed,
The motherland will remember, the blood that you shed.
In the hearts of your comrades, and your countrymen too,
You'll live on forever, in the red, white, and blue.

29. William A Sangma

In northeastern state a man stood,
A leader bold, with vision good.
William A. Sangma, his name renowned,
In the heart of the hills, his legacy crowned.
With lurking stride and noble grace,
He led his people in every place.
From Tura's hills to Shillong's breeze,
He championed tribal rights with ease.
Chief Minister he, with wisdom's light,
Guided Meghalaya through day and night.
In governance strong, he took his stand,
For progress and peace across the land.
Advocate of tribes, their voice he raised,
In halls of power, where justice blazed.
For tribal rights, he fought with might,
In every battle, for truth and right.
A leader true now lies in shroud,
His deeds echo throughout abode of cloud,
A ray of hope in a man so kind,
William A. Sangma, in memory enshrined,

Though he may rest in fields of green,
His spirit, his vision, forever keen.
In Meghalaya's heart, his name shall ring,

A tribute to him, we forever sing.
In William A. Sangma's honor, we say,
Thank you for lighting our path each day.
Your legacy lives, in the hearts that beat,
In the northeast's story, forever sweet.

30. Tihar

In the vibrant and lively Indian culture,
Nepali hearts find a festive allure.
Tihar, a radiant jewel in the year's embrace,
Bringing joy and light to every space.
As the autumn breeze carries a whisper of cheer,
Nepali homes glow with lamps so dear.
Beautiful lights in bustling streets and lanes,
The spirit of Tihar joyously reigns.
Each day of Tihar holds its own delight,
A symphony of rituals, a luminous sight.
From Kaag Tihar with crows in the morning sun,
To Bhai Tika, sibling bonds forever spun.
Marigold garlands adorn doorways with grace,
As homes are adorned, a sacred space.
Colorful rangolis bedeck the floor,
Welcoming luck and blessings galore.
Deities are honored with fervent devotion,
Amidst chants and prayers, a heartfelt emotion.
Goddess Laxmi, embodiment of wealth and light,
Bestows her blessings, shining bright.
In India's melting pot of diversity,
Nepali culture blooms in unity.
Tihar, a festival of love and mirth,
Bringing together hearts from every birth.

Though miles may stretch between land and kin,
Tihar binds them close, from within.
In the glow of lamps and laughter's embrace,
Nepali spirits are high in every place.

31. Kul Puja

In Darjeeling, beneath the Kanchenjunga peak,
Where heritage whispers and tradition speak,
Lies a ritual cherished old and true,
Kul Puja, a bond between Him and you.
Gathered around the hearth, in reverence we stand,
Ancestral spirits, a guiding hand.
With offerings of flowers, fruits so sweet,
They honor our roots, in each heart beat.
Kul Devta, guardian of their clan,
In His presence, their spirits expand.
Blessings they seek, for their family tree,
Grant them prosperity, harmony, and glee.
Through generations, their light shines bright,
Symbol of love, in the darkest night.
In this sacred union, past and present entwine,
As they honour their ancestors, in this hymn divine.
So let them sing, let their voices soar,
In praise of those who've gone before.
Kul Puja, a culture woven with care,
Binding them close, in a bond rare.

32. Kong Nah's Kitchen

Admist the hills in Khasi land,
Where kong Nah's heart and kitchen stand,
A feast of flavors, rich and grand,
In every dish, a story planned.
Rice, the foundation, pure and white,
Binds the meal from dawn till night.
With meat, the pride of Khasi fare,
Pork and chicken, flavors rare.
Jadoh sings with spice and heat,
Rice and meat in union sweet.
Tungrymbai's the fermented grace,
A taste of tradition, time to embrace.
Doh-Neiiong, with sesame's kiss,
A savory symphony, hard to miss.
Each bite, a journey, flavors bloom,
In Khasi kitchens, in every room.
Kwai, the betel, shared with cheer,
A bond of friendship, ever near.
Chutneys, pickles, vibrant and bold,
A burst of flavors that her foods hold.
So let us savour, let us dine,
On Khasi food, a treasure divine.
In every bite, a tale unfolds,
Of culture, heritage, and stories old.

33. Mayong: Whispered With Fear

In the shadows of Assam's secret land,
Lies a village steeped in tales so grand.
Mayong, its name whispered with fear,
Where mystic whispers and legends leer.
In the heart of this ancient domain,
Echoes of magic in the winds remain.
Mayongia Tantra, the ancient art,
Spins spells and potions, weaving hearts.
Beneath the boughs of the whispering trees,
Whispers of sorcery dance on the breeze.
Legends speak of powers unseen,
Where reality blurs and dreams convene.
Strange are the tales that Mayong tells,
Of vanishing souls and enchanted spells.
In the twilight's embrace, secrets unfold,
In this village where mysteries behold.
Yet beyond the shroud of darkness and dread,
Lies a tapestry of history, richly spread.
Mayong, a cradle of culture and lore,
Where tales of magic and truth adore.
So wanderer, tread softly through Mayong's streets,
Where enchantment and reality discreet.

For in this village, where shadows play,
Legends linger, casting their sway.

34. Nepali Attire a Symbol Grand

In Gorkhaland where the hills touch the sky,
Where Nepali spirits soar up high,
Daura-Suruwal, with colors bold,
A tale of heritage, proudly told.
With closed-neck shirts and trousers wide,
Men stride with grace, their culture's pride.
Bundi vests and Dhaka topi adorn,
Their attire speaks of mountains born.
Gunyo Cholo, in colour so bright,
Adorns Nepali women with delight.
Pothu skirts swish with every stride,
As Patuka shawls their beauty hide.
In Sikkim's hills and Darjeeling's breeze,
In Assam's valleys and Bengal's trees,
Nepali attire, a symbol grand,
Of unity and pride in every land.
With earrings gleaming, and bangles bright,
Their traditional dress a graceful sight.
In festivals and weddings, they dance and sing,
Their heritage alive in everything.
So let us celebrate, with hearts aglow,
The Nepali attire, with reverence bestowed.

For in each thread, a story's spun,
Of resilience, culture, and unity won.

35. Nongjrong

In Nongjrong hills, where clouds do roam,
A hidden gem, a traveler's tome.
Where Umngot's river whispers low,
And sun-kissed valleys in splendor glow.
Upon the hill, where shadows fade,
The Nongjrong View Point, where dreams cascade.
Before the dawn, when darkness wanes,
The sky ablaze with fiery veins.
With each sunrise, a symphony unfolds,
As misty veils the landscape holds.
Green hills stretch far, in gentle sway,
In Nongjrong's beauty, time drifts away.
From Shillong's heart, a journey start,
Through winding roads and nature's art
To Nongjrong's haven, where peace reside,
And beauty's secrets are softly bide.
So come, dear traveler, venture near,
To Nongjrong's realm, without a fear.
Where clouds embrace, and mountain sings
In Nongjrong's heart, let your soul take wings.

36. Sattriya Dance Finds its Grace

In the land of the blue hills where rivers flow,
Sattriya dance, its tales bestow.
A dance of devotion, pure and bright,
In Sankardeva's divine light.
From Sattra's walls, the dance does rise,
A tribute to the sacred skies.
In graceful movements, stories told,
Of legends ancient, hearts enfold.
Costumes vibrant, makeup bold,
Intricate patterns, stories unfold.
Mukha Pravesh, with reverence deep,
A spiritual journey, for hearts to keep.
With every step, a prayer is said,
To gods and goddesses, hearts are led.
In rhythmic beats, the music sways,
As dancers weave their mystic ways.
Nitya, Nritya, Natya too,
Expressions myriad, dreams pursue.
In Krishna's love, Radha's embrace,
Sattriya dance, finds its grace.
Accompanied by melodies sweet,
Traditional tunes, the dancers meet.

With khol and tal, the rhythm flows,
In Sattriya's dance, devotion glows.
Recognized as classical, pure and true,
Sattriya dance, in Assam's view.
A heritage cherished, for all to see,
In every movement, history's plea.
So let the rhythms of Sattriya ring,
In every heart, let the dance sing.
A tribute to culture, tradition's art,
Sattriya dance, forever in our heart.

37. Dashain's Spirit

In Darjeeling hills where mountains rise,
Dashain's spirit fills the skies.
A festival of joy and light,
A celebration, pure and bright.

Ghatasthapana marks the start,
As seeds are sown, with hopeful heart.
Barley sprouts, a symbol true,
Of blessings new, for me and you.

Throughout the days, we worship Durga,
In all her forms, her grace we nurture.
With prayers and offerings, sincere and deep,
Her divine blessings, we earnestly seek.

Family reunions, laughter rings,
As loved ones gather, hearts take wings.
Elders bless with tika's mark,
A symbol of love, through light and dark.

Feasting on selroti and a grand buffet,
With flavors rich, in every way.
Spirits high in skies so blue,
A symbol of joy, in all we do.

But Dashain's spirit goes beyond,
To acts of kindness, we respond.
In charity's embrace, we find our call,
To spread the joy, to one and all.

So let the drums of Dashain beat,
In every heart, in every street.
A festival of love and bliss,
Dashain's gathering we never miss.

38. Lachit Borphukan His Valour Alive

In the Land of the Red River, where legends thrive,
Lachit Borphukan, his valor alive.
A warrior born, of noble name,
In history's annals, he earned his fame.
From youth, he honed his martial skill,
With courage ablaze, and iron will.
To defend his land, he took his stand,
A hero born, to protect his land.
As Mughal shadows loomed afar,
Lachit's resolve burned like a star.
Against the tide of invaders' might,
He led his troops, in the fateful fight.

At Saraighat's banks, they made their stand,
Defending Assam's sacred land.
With strategy bold and tactics keen,
They faced the foe, in battles unseen.

Outnumbered, but undaunted still,
Lachit's warriors fought with skill.
Through rivers' flow and arrows' rain,
They held the line, their homeland to regain.

With victory won, their banners flew,
Assam's spirit, forever true.
In Lachit's name, they sing their praise,
For his courage and valor, in ancient days.

Though time may pass, and empires fall,
Lachit Borphukan stands tall.
A beacon of hope, for all to see,
In Assam's land, for eternity.

39. Bagurrumba's Grace

Sunlight dappled, leaves alight,
Drums beat a rhythm, taking flight.
The Gamsa sways, a colorful dress,
Dokhona bright, a woman's bless.
Bagurumba's grace, a silent song,
Mimicking birds on a gentle storm.
The fluted Horiga fills the air,
Myths and legends, a rich history to share.
Bwisagu's joy, a harvest's call,
Thanking Bathou, who gives them all.
Bodo culture, wild and free,
Forever flowing, eternally.

40. Flows the Mighty Brahmaputra

In the plains of Assam, where lovely people dwell,
Flows the mighty Brahmaputra's spell.
From Himalayan heights, it takes its start,
A river of strength, with beating heart.
Through rugged gorges and valleys deep,
It carves its path, a journey to keep.
A force of nature, relentless and free,
The Brahmaputra roars, for all to see.
From Tibet's peaks, it rushes down,
A torrent of life, it wears no crown.
Through Arunachal's wild embrace,
It rushes forth, with untamed grace.
In Assam's plains, it spreads its might,
A lifeline for millions, shining bright.
The land it nourishes, the crops it feeds,
In Brahmaputra's flow, prosperity breeds.
But with its might, it knows no rest,
Its floods and rages, at nature's behest.
Its currents swirl, with fearsome roar,
A force of nature, forever more.
Yet in its depths, a beauty lies,
A river of dreams under the blue skies.

A symbol of resilience, through the years,
The mighty Brahmaputra, calms our fears.

41. The Gorkha's Tale

In the plains of Assam where Brahmaputra flow,
The Gorkha community's tales do grow.
From distant hills and valleys fair,
They bring their heritage, rich and rare.
With footsteps bold, they blessed the land,
From hills and valleys to Assam's strand.
In search of dreams, in search of hope,
In Assam's embrace, they learned to cope.
In Dibrugarh's fields, and Tinsukia's shade,
Their stories bloom, in sunlight laid.
From Golaghat's hills to Sivasagar's pride,
The Gorkha spirit, cannot be denied.
Dashain's drums and Tihar's light,
Echo through the day and night.
Maghe Sankranti's melodious song,
In Assam's heart, they do belong.
In Nepali tongues, their tales are told,
Of courage, honor, and stories old.
Assamese whispers, blend and twine,
In unity, their smiles shine.
From army barracks to tea estate,
In every corner, they create.
With toil and sweat, they carve their way,
In Assam's canvas, they do stay.

Through organizations, voices rise,
To claim their place under northeastern skies.
Citizenship, rights, and identity more,
In Assam's story, they implore.
So let their tales, forever be,
In Assam's lap, under peepal tree.
The Gorkha values full of love,
Compassionate like a gentle dove.

42. Darjeeling Tea Garden

In Darjeeling's gardens, where whispers dwell,
Tales unfold, in misty spell.
Amidst the tea leaves, stories bloom,
In nature's embrace, tales resume.
Romantic whispers beneath moon's glow,
Love's tender dance, in verdant flow.
Two hearts entwined, amidst the green,
In Darjeeling's gardens, love is seen.
Through corridors of time, history weaves,
Colonial echoes, amidst the leaves.
Legacy of labor, struggles told,
In Darjeeling's gardens, stories old.
Families intertwined, generations strong,
Roots run deep, in hills where they belong.
Dreams and conflicts, aspirations high,
In Darjeeling's gardens, life's sigh.
Mystery shrouded in mist's embrace,
Secrets hidden, in time and space.
Intrigue unfolds, amidst the breeze,
In Darjeeling's gardens, whispers tease.
Social realities, stark and clear,
Labor's toil, in shadows near.
Inequality's tale, amidst the green,
In Darjeeling's gardens, truth unseen.

So let the stories, in gardens reside,
In Darjeeling's beauty, they'll abide.
Through our own eyes, we'll explore,
The beauty of the tea garden more and more.

43. Bihe

Among the Gorkhas, where traditions reign,
Marriage takes forms, a varied terrain.
Let's wander through the paths they tread,
Where love and customs gently spread.
a) Chori Biha - Theft Marriage:
In whispers soft, beneath moon's light,
A love blooms sudden, out of sight.
He steals her heart, a daring feat,
In secrecy, their vows they greet.
No time for courtship's gentle sway,
Their love unfolds in night's array.
With whispered vows, they flee the fold,
In love's embrace, their tale is told.
b) Zari Biha - Marriage by Paying Penalty:
A woman's heart, a precious prize,
Her consent sought in lover's eyes.
To pay the price, a penalty fair,
In love's pursuit, they boldly dare.
From hand to hand, the coins exchange,
As vows are sworn, their hearts arrange.
With honor paid, a new bond forms,
In love's embrace, their spirit warms.
c) Senzi Zari Biha - Widow Marriage:
In shadows cast by sorrow's plight,

A widow finds her guiding light.
No social chains to hold her down,
In love's embrace, a new love's crown.
With solemn grace, she finds her way,
In widowhood, a brighter day.
With compensation, honor shown,
In love's embrace, she finds her own.
d) Magi Biha - Arranged Marriage:
In whispers shared under the starry skies,
Two families meet, with hopeful eyes.
With mutual consent, the knot is tied,
In love exchanged and their hearts allied.
Arranged with care, by kin's decree,
A union forged, in unity.
With blessings shared, their journey starts,
In love's embrace, they share their hearts.
In Gorkha community, love's different forms,
From stolen glances to vows sworn.
In every union, love's sweet refrain,
In a lovely union, they find their gain.

44. Anjaw Takes its Flight

In the land of Mishi Hills, where mountains touch the sky,
Lies a legend whispered, where spirits soar and fly.
Anjaw, they call it, a tale of mystic might,
Where the legendary bird takes its celestial flight.
Anjaw, the messenger, with feathers bright and bold,
In the ancient lore of Mishmi, its story is told.
From the peaks of the Himalayas to the valleys deep,
Anjaw soars, its secrets to keep.
With wings that span the heavens, it glides on winds of fate,
Across the land of Arunachal, where legends congregate.
Through whispers of the forests and songs of the streams,
Anjaw carries messages, beyond mortal dreams.
In the hearts of the Mishmi, its presence is revered,
For Anjaw brings blessings, in every flight it steered.
In the legend of Anjaw, where mysteries shine,
A symbol of grace, in the land divine.
So let the legend of Anjaw, in tales unfold,
A tribute to the spirit, forever bold.
For in the skies of Mishi Hills, where Anjaw takes its flight
To protect the lovely land, with all its bravery and might.

45. Tripura Sundari : A Goddess Divine

In Tripura's realm, where legends weave,
Lies a tale of grace, where spirits cleave.
Tripura Sundari, a goddess divine,
In myth and in lore, her virtues shine.
Born of beauty, with a heart so pure,
Tripura Sundari, forever sure.
The mixed culture brings delight,
She reigns supreme, in soft moonlight.
With eyes like stars, and a smile so bright,
Tripura Sundari, in ethereal light.
She walks among mortals, with gentle grace,
A goddess of love, in every place.
In temples adorned, with offerings rare,
Devotees gather, their hearts laid bare.
For Tripura Sundari, with compassion so true,
Listens to prayers, like morning dew.
With the passage of time, her legend weaves,
A ray of hope, in shadowed eaves.
For Tripura Sundari, forever shall be,
A symbol of beauty for eternity.

46. Legend of Khonoma

Among the Nagas of hilly terrace,
Lies a legend that belongs to their race.
Khonoma, they call it, a village of lore,
Tales of valour for us to explore.
In the shadow of mountains, unknown mystery,
Khonoma stands proud, creating the history.
A bastion of strength, against invaders' might,
Its people defended, with gutsy fight.
The legend speaks of battles, waged long ago,
When foes descended, like a torrential flow.
But Khonoma's warriors, with spirit unyielding,
Stood firm and resolute, their destiny wielding.
Through valleys and hills, their battle cry rang,
As they fought and their freedom sang.
With arrows and spears, they held the line,
Against tyranny's grasp, their resolve did shine.
Generations have passed, yet the tales remain,
In Khonoma's spirit, where courage sustain.
For in the memoirs of time, its story is told,
Of a village of heroes, resilient and bold.
So let us honor Khonoma from their folktales,
For its legacy lives on in their trail.
In the heart of Naga Hills, where mountains loom,
Khonoma's legend continues to bloom.

47. Chungliyimti Found His Home

In the heart of Naga Hills, where tales abound,
Lies a legend of bravery, profound.
Chungliyimti, they call him, a hero bold,
Whose story through generations is told.
With a heart of courage and eyes aflame,
He stood against darkness, never tame.
In the land of Nagas, where spirits roam,
Chungliyimti found his home.
Through forests deep and valleys wide,
He journeyed forth, with honor as his guide.
In battles fierce, with demons dark,
He fought for his people, left his mark.
With spear in hand and spirit pure,
Chungliyimti faced trials sure.
From mountain peaks to far and wide,
He braved the storm, never to hide.
In the blindest of night, under a starlit sky,
Chungliyimti's legend will never die.
For in his courage, we find our soul,
A lantern of hope, shining bold.
So let us remember him in the stories told,
The legend of Chungliyimti, brave and bold.

For in his valor, we find our might,
Hold the story in your heart with delight.

48. Pahsyntiew

In the midst of the wettest land,
Where waterfalls cascade, so grand,
Wonderful Khasi folklore I knew,
Of Pahsyntiew in the morning dew.
She dwelt among the misty spray,
Where rainbows dance and sunlight play,
With hair of silver and eyes so bright,
She guards the falls, in morning light.
From rocky cliffs, she watches the flow,
As waters rush and dreams bestow,
A guardian spirit, pure and fair,
Pahsyntiew's beauty of utmost rare.
In the whispers of the falls, her voice is heard,
A melody sweet, like the song of a bird,
She sings of legends, of tales untold,
In the language of water, pure and bold.
Oh, Pahsyntiew, soul divine,
In your embrace, a sacred shrine,
Guide us through the mist and spray,
As we wander, on our way.
For in your waters, we find our source,
A timeless bond, a sacred force,
Pahsyntiew, spirit on the calls,
Protecting and preserving the waterfalls.

49. Ka Nam

In the village, where shieldmaiden reside,
Lies a tale of bravery, in their own pride.
Ka Nam, they call her, with courage untamed,
In the pages of folklore, her glory proclaimed.
With eyes like fire and a heart of gold,
Ka Nam roamed the forests, wild and bold.
She walked with purpose, through the whispering trees,
A champion of justice, in the mountain breeze.
In the land of myths, where khasis dwell,
Ka Nam faced challenges fierce and fell.
From cunning demons to spirits of the night,
She stood unwavering, in the face of fright.
With wisdom as her weapon, and kindness her shield,
Ka Nam ventured forth, her fate revealed.
Through trials and tribulations, she forged her name,
A heroine of legend, in Khasi fame.
So let us remember, in tales untold,
The legacy of Ka Nam, brave and bold.
For in her courage, we find our own,
In the heart of the khasis, forever known.

50. U Thlen

In the misty hills of Meghalaya fair,
Where legends dance in the cool, crisp air,
Lies a tale of old, both dark and deep,
Of a serpent's slumber, its secrets to keep.
U Thlen, they call it, a creature of might,
With scales like shadows, and eyes alight.
In the heart of the jungle, it coils and waits,
A guardian of secrets, at the forest's gates.
With venomous breath and a hunger dire,
U Thlen lurks, its flames of desire.
For it feasts on souls, the story untold,
A darkness within, a legend bold.
But brave were the warriors of olden days,
Who faced the beast in the moon's soft gaze.
With swords of courage and hearts of steel,
They vowed to vanquish, to break the seal.
Through valleys deep and mountains high,
They found the serpent and took a sigh.
With chants of valor and prayers divine,
They sought to banish its treacherous sign.
In the final clash, under the moon's pale gleam,
The warriors fought, a fearless team.
With a mighty blow and a righteous cry,
They struck U Thlen, and watched it die.

But legends linger, in the misty air,
Of U Thlen's wrath, of the serpent's lair.
For though it sleeps in the depths below,
Its tale lives on, in the hearts that know.
So let us heed the lessons learned,
From the folklore of U Thlen earned.
For in darkness lies both fear and light,
And in bravery, khasis find their might.

51. Jhuma

In Himalayan hills, where mountains kiss the sky,
Lies a tradition under the divine eye.
Jhuma, they call it, a practice old and true,
Where girls become goddesses, in red and blue.
In far-western lands, where tales are told,
Young maidens are chosen, pure as gold.
They adorn the throne, as living divine,
Believed to hold blessings, like sweetest wine.
Their footsteps sacred, their laughter bright,
As they reign over villages, day and night.
With flowers in their hair, and innocence so clear,
They bring hope and solace, dispelling every fear.
Yet time takes its toll, and girlhood wanes,
Jhuma must return to earthly plains.
She sheds her divine form, with a tender sigh,
A mortal once again descends to die.
But in memories lingering, her presence stays,
A symbol of faith, in mysterious ways.
For Jhuma's tale, though strange it may seem,
Reflects the beauty of a timeless dream.
In Sikkimise hearts, where traditions dance,
Jhuma's spirit lives on, in every glance.
For she embodies purity, in its purest hue,
A reminder of divinity, in me and you.

52. A Chik Embrace

In A chik embrace, where beauty thrills,
Lie the Garo land, with dwarfy hills.
Where Simsang flows and forests dance,
In nature's lap, we find romance.
Amidst the green, the Garo tribe resides,
With traditions old and cultural tides.
Their drums resound, their dances swirl,
In celebration of nature's unfurl.
From Nokrek's heights to Siju's caves,
Nature's wonders, the land enslaves.
In orange groves and rice fields wide,
The people toil with joy and pride.
Tourists wander, their hearts to fill,
With sights and sounds of Garo's thrill.
In Wangala's joy and Nokrek's might,
They find in Garo a pure delight.
Yet challenges loom, in shadows cast,
In need of roads and progress fast.
But amidst it all, hope prevails,
In Garo's heart, the spirit sails.
For in this land of hills and streams,
Lies the essence of nature's dreams.
In Garo's embrace, we find our worth,
A treasure trove of Mother Earth.

53. Lapang's Legacy Lights the Way

In Meghalaya's Ri Bhoi, beside the road,
Lies the tale of Lapang, in the 'bhois' abode.
A leader, revered, in the land of his birth,
A ray of hope, for all souls on earth.
With wisdom deep and vision clear,
He led with courage, without fear.
Through valleys and forests, his voice did ring,
For the people's welfare, he took the wing.
From humble beginnings, he rose to might,
Guiding Meghalaya through darkest night.
In governance and service, his legacy shines,
A testament to strength in trying times.
With unity as his guiding star,
He bridged divides, near and far.
Ka jingshisha ka jaitbynriew the noble quest
In his leadership, Meghalaya found rest.
His age is now taking a toll,
He still serves with his attitude bold
D.D. Lapang the true man,
He works for the people even in disdain.

54. Purno Sangma : A Beacon of Light

In Garo hills, where great hornbill takes flight,
Stood Purno Sangma, a ray of light.
With vision high where people were gazed,
He forged a path though the life was mazed.
A son of the soil, tribal pride in his veins,
He fought for the rights, amidst life's strains.
From Garo hills to khasi hills, his voice resound,
For the marginalized, his efforts were profound.
In the corridors of power, he stood tall,
A leader true, heeding the tribal call.
Chief Minister, MP, a statesman grand,
In service to Meghalaya, he took his stand.
Bridging divides, he sought to unite,
Empowering youth, with futures bright.
In classrooms and fields, his legacy gleams,
Nurturing dreams, beyond the streams.
Roads he paved, to progress's door,
With infrastructure, he aimed to soar.
Healthcare, education, in his sight,
For every Meghalayan, life and delight.
Though time may pass, and seasons change,
In our hearts his memory remains,

Purno Sangma's works we will forever cherish.
Under whose leadership, the state flourished.

55. Mahi

In the realm of cricket's grand domain,
There shines a star, a legend's reign.
Dhoni, the captain, cool and composed,
In the cricket history, his name enclosed.
With gloves of lightning, behind the stumps,
He danced with grace, in cricket's trumps.
His reflexes swift, his presence bold,
In cricket's theatre, a story he told.
In the crucible of pressure, he stood tall,
A leader supreme, inspiring all.
With victories cherished, and trophies raised high,
He painted the canvas of Indian sky.
In the twilight's glow, and under the sun's heat,
His bat did sing, a victory sweet.
As a finisher supreme, he scripted delight,
Guiding India home, into the night.
Beyond the boundary, his influence soared,
A mentor, a guide, revered and adored.
In the hearts of millions, his legacy gleams,
A beacon of hope, in dreams and schemes.
In the span of time, his tale is spun,
Of battles fought, and victories won.
Dhoni, the maestro, forever enshrined,
In cricket's lore, his perfection defined.

56. Jallikattu

In Tamil Nadu's golden land, where Anna rise,
Lies a spectacle of courage under sunlit skies.
Jallikattu, where man and bull unite,
In a dance of valour, fierce fight.
Beneath the heavens, the crowd gathers near,
With hearts that beat in rhythm, devoid of fear.
The bull, a symbol of strength and grace,
Challenges the brave in this ancient race.
With horns adorned with coins, it strides with pride,
As fearless souls step forth, by tradition tied.
In the arena's dust, where legends are made,
The spirit of bravery shall never fade.
With muscles tense and eyes ablaze,
Man and beast engage in this timeless maze.
The thunderous roar of the charging bull,
Echoes the courage of those who are full.
Amidst the chaos, there's a silent bond,
Between man and beast, in a contest fond.
For in this dance of strength and might,
Resides the essence of honor, burning bright.
Though debates may rage, and controversies fly,
Jallikattu remains under the vast Tamil sky.
A testament to heritage, brave and true,
A timeless tradition, for me and you.

57. Exuberant Garo Heritage

In western Meghalaya where Garos live,
A culture exuberant, with stories to weave.
Amongst lush valleys, where rivers play,
The Garo essence dances, come what may.
Garo heritage full of life,
They are strong in all they strive.
With Dakmanda and Gando, they adorn,
Their colorful attire, from dusk till dawn.
Music fills the air, with rhythms sweet,
As dancers move, to the Wangala's beat.
In colorful attire, they whirl and twirl,
Their steps narrating, an ancient swirl.
In Garo land, beliefs run deep,
Nature's spirits, they fondly keep.
With rituals and rites, they pay homage fair,
To ancestors' wisdom, in the air.
Artisans skilled, their crafts they ply,
Bamboo weavers, under the cloudy sky.
Pottery, carving, their hands create,
Treasures of heritage, they decorate.
From rice fields green, to river's bend,
Garo cuisine, a feast to send.
With fish and meat, and flavors bold,
Their culinary tale, forever told.

Through Den Bilsia and Rongchu gala (Festivals)
The Garo festivals, sing Hosanna.
With joy and laughter, they celebrate,
Their culture's essence, ever innate.
Oh, Garo culture, in Meghalaya's mart,
A symphony of traditions, a living art.
In every dress and in every song,
The Garo heritage mesmerizing and strong.

58. Embracing the World They Find Their Way

In the villages where Gorkhas reside,
An identity crisis, they silently confide.
Bound by their heritage, yet torn apart,
Between two worlds, they find their heart.
Citizens of India, with Gorkha bloodline,
Their identity complex got their bravery malign.
Their culture rich, their roots run deep,
Yet in the history of India, they often seek.
Caught between loyalties, they navigate,
The complexities of identity, they contemplate.
Indian by citizenship, Gorkha by pride,
Their sense of self, a journey to stride.
Their language, their customs, a source of pride,
Yet often misunderstood, cast aside.
In the melting pot of diversity, they seek,
A space to thrive, a voice to speak.
Yet amidst the struggle, they find strength,
In unity and resilience, they go to lengths.
For the Gorkha people, with hearts so true,
Their identity crisis, they'll journey through.
Embracing world, they find their way,
In India's heritage, they proudly stay.

For in their diversity, they find their might,
The Gorkha life, a dazzling light.

59. Courage of Gorkha Soldiers

In the shadow of mountains, bold and proud,
Stands the Gorkha soldier, valiant and unbowed.
From the northeast's rugged hills, they hail with might,
Guardians of honor, in the nation's fight.
With khukuris gleaming, in the sun's warm glow,
They march with purpose, wherever they go.
Their courage unmatched, their loyalty true,
In service to the nation, they stand resolute.
Through valleys and forests, they tread the land,
Protecting the borders, with a steady hand.
In every battle, they face with grace,
Their valor and sacrifice, leave a lasting trace.
From the heights of Siachen, to the plains below,
The Gorkha soldier, in every foe they overthrow.
With discipline and honor, they stand tall,
A testament to duty, answering the call.
In the heart of every Gorkha, beats a flame,
For country and comrades, they stake their claim.
Their legacy written, in tales of glory,
The Gorkha soldier, an everlasting story.

60. Mawsynram

In the realm of Meghalaya, where the clouds sway,
Lies Mawsynram, where raindrops play.
A place of wonder, where skies weep,
In the embrace of mist, secrets to keep.
Rain-soaked hills, cloaked in green,
Mawsynram's beauty, a sight unseen.
With every drop, a whispered tale,
Of monsoon's dance, beyond the veil.
In Mawsynram's heart, the rainbows bloom,
Painting the sky, chasing the gloom.
Amidst the downpour, life finds a way,
In the rhythm of rain, night and day.
The sound of rain, a soothing lullaby,
In Mawsynram's arms, under the sky.
A symphony of droplets, a gentle hum,
In nature's chorus, we all become one.
In the rainiest place on Earth, where waters flow,
Mawsynram's spirit, forever aglow.
A testament to nature's power and grace,
In Mawsynram's arms, we find our place.

61. Abundant Cultures in the Shillong Hills

In Shillong's hills, where dreams take flight,
Abundant cultures, bathed in light.
Khasis, Garos, Bengalis, and more,
In harmony they dwell, by Shillong's shore.
The Khasis, with their matrilineal grace,
Their customs and traditions, they proudly embrace.
The Garos, guardians of ancient lore,
Their rhythms and melodies, forever soar.
Bengalis, with their vibrant hues,
Their literature and arts, a muse.
Nepalis, with their mountain's call,
Their resilience and spirit, standing tall.
Punjabis, with their zest for life,
Their warmth and laughter, amidst the strife.
And others from distant lands afar,
Each adding their own, to Shillong's star.
In Shillong's streets, a symphony plays,
A fusion of cultures, in countless ways.
Temples, mosques, and churches stand,
Symbols of faith, across the land.
In markets bustling, with colors bright,
A kaleidoscope of sounds, in the night.

The aroma of spices, fills the air,
A feast for the senses, everywhere.
Yet amidst the diversity, a common thread,
A spirit of unity, in words unsaid.
For in Shillong's heart, there lies a bond,
A shared humanity, forever fond.
Oh, Shillong, city of peace and love,
A testament to what we're made of.
May your spirit of harmony, forever thrive,
In the fabric of cultures, you so beautifully revive.

62. Humanity's Essence

In the rush of the modern age, we race,
Lost in the chaos, we've misplaced,
The tender touch, the empathetic gaze,
As we navigate life's frenzied maze.
Technology's allure, a double-edged sword,
Connecting us all, yet leaving hearts ignored.
In the glow of screens, we lose sight,
Of the souls around us, hidden from light.
In the pursuit of progress, we've left behind,
The simple joys, the ties that bind.
Humanity's essence, slipping away,
In a world consumed by power's sway.
Greed and ambition, driving us apart,
Fracturing bonds, corroding the heart.
As we chase wealth and fame's elusive gleam,
We lose touch with what it means to dream.
Yet in the midst of this darkened night,
A flicker of hope, a guiding light.
For deep within, the ember still burns,
A yearning for love, for peace, for turns.
Let us pause in the rush, and listen close,
To the whispers of the heart, the silent prose.
For in reclaiming our humanity's song,
We find the strength to right the wrong.

So let compassion be our guiding star,
In this modern world, no matter how far.
For in the end, it's our humanity,
That will lead us home, to unity.

63. Darjeeling Hills

In the Himalayas, where sunbirds take flight,
Lies Darjeeling, a vision of pure delight.
Where snow-capped peaks kiss the morning sun,
And tea gardens glisten, when the day is done.
Majestic Kanchenjunga, towering high,
A sentinel of beauty, against the sky.
Its snow-clad peaks, a sight to behold,
In Darjeeling's embrace, a story untold.
Rolling hills adorned in green,
Tea gardens stretch, a tranquil scene.
Rows of bushes, neatly arrayed,
Where tea leaves dance, in the breeze they're swayed.
Along winding tracks, the Toy Train chugs,
Through valleys and forests, it gently tugs.
A journey of wonder, a ride to cherish,
In Darjeeling's hills, where memories flourish.

Flowers bloom in hues so rare,
Rhododendrons, magnolias, fill the air.
Birds sing sweet melodies, in nature's embrace,
A symphony of life, a sacred space.
Monasteries perched on hillsides steep,
Where prayer flags flutter, in winds that sweep.
Buddhist chants, in tranquil tones,

Echo through valleys, to unknown zones.
Colonial charm, amidst the mist,
Cobbled streets, bygone era kissed.
A legacy of yesteryears, in every brick and stone,
In Darjeeling's streets, history's throne.
Amidst the hustle and bustle, a peaceful refrain,
Darjeeling's hills, where souls find gain.
In nature's bounty, in cultural pride,
In every moment, beauty resides.
Oh, Darjeeling Hills, a treasure rare,
In your embrace, we find solace fair.
A sanctuary of dreams, where spirits find peace,
In Darjeeling's hills, serenity's release.

64. Beidingkhlam

In the Hills cultural richness roam,
Lies a festival, Beidingkhlam, our home.
Where rhythms beat and colors gleam,
A celebration, like a radiant dream.

Amidst the hills, in July's phase,
The village stirs, with joy and grace.
For Beidingkhlam has come again,
To wash away sorrow, to banish pain.

With Rath in hand, the villagers sway,
To the river's edge, they make their way.
U Lei Shillong, hear our plea,
Bless our land, set our spirits free.

Ka Pomblang Nongkrem, the dance begins,
Feathers and drums, amidst the din.
Men of Pnar, with steps so bold,
Their stories are expressed, in dance untold.

Sports and games, in fields they play,
Football matches, archery's display.
Tug of War and wooden pole climb,
A testament to strength, across time.

Oh, Bêidingkhlam, festival grand,
In Pnar hills, you stand.
A celebration of culture and lore,
Forever treasured our spirits soar.

So let us gather, in joyful throng,
Sing the festival's timeless song.
For in Beidingkhlam, Jaintias sway,
In unity and hope, day by day.

65. In the Shadow of the Himalayas

In the shadow of the Himalayas' grandeur,
Lies a land of beauty, culture, and ardor.
Where the Gorkhas roam with pride,
In the valleys where dreams abide.

From Darjeeling's hills to Sikkim's embrace,
Nepali hearts beat with timeless grace.
Their language, a melody in the breeze,
Echoes of home, across the seas.

In temples adorned with marigold's hue,
Hindu gods and goddesses come into view.
And Buddhist chants fill the mountain air,
With prayers for peace, beyond compare.

Momos steam in the bustling street,
A taste of home, so savory and sweet.
Thukpa warms the soul on a chilly night,
In the glow of lanterns, burning bright.

With sarangi's song and madal's beat,
Nepali music, so pure and sweet.

Dancers whirl in colorful attire,
Their feet telling stories of joy and desire.

Thangka paintings, a window to the divine,
Capturing moments frozen in time.
Craftsmen carve tales in wood and stone,
Their artistry, a legacy to be known.

In Dashain's light, families unite,
In laughter, love, and pure delight.
Underneath the moon's gentle gaze,
They dance and sing, in ancient ways.

Oh, Nepali culture, rich and grand,
A mosaic woven by skilled hands.
In North Bengal, you find your home,
In hearts that beat with love alone.

66. So Let Us Dance the Khasi Way

In Meghalaya's lively terrace,
Where Khasi hills hold ancient grace,
Lies a tribe, proud and free,
In nature's embrace, they dance with glee.

Their language sings with ancient lores,
Echoes during the daily chores.
Matrilineal bonds, strong and true,
Guide their steps, in all they do.

Amidst mist-kissed valleys, they dwell,
Where living bridges weave their spell.
Roots reaching out, across the stream,
A testament to dreams, a timeless seam.

Nongkrem's dance, in November's light,
Honors the land, with all their might.
Nature's bounty, their hearts entwine,
In rhythm and rhyme, beneath the pine.

With rice and pork, they break the bread,
Hospitality, by their hands spread.

Jadoh's warmth, Dohneiiong's delight,
Flavors that linger, through the night.

Oh, Khasi tribe, in Meghalaya bold,
A story with a heart of gold.
In your land, where beauty thrives,
We find our souls, forever alive.

So let us dance the Khasi way,
Underneath the sun's golden ray.
For in their culture, we find our art,
A symphony of love, in every heart.

67. Umiam Lake

In Meghalaya's embrace, serene and still,
Lies Umiam Lake, a tranquil thrill.
Also known as Barapani, a gem so bright,
Reflecting the heavens, a beacon of light.
Nestled in hills, just north of Shillong's embrace,
A reservoir of dreams, in a tranquil space.
Born from the Umiam river's gentle flow,
In the early '60s, its story did grow.
Mornings awakened with a gentle mist,
As dawn's first light, the lake has kissed.
Whispers of dawn, a soft embrace,
As the lake stirs with morning grace.
Beneath the canopy of stars at night,
Umiam Lake gleams with celestial light.
A collection of stars, a silent choir,
Reflecting in the lake's tranquil attire.
Oh, Umiam Lake, a jewel so fair,
In the northeast rare, beyond compare.
A haven of peace, where spirits roam free,
In nature's embrace, for eternity.
May the waves of Umiam, gentle and true,
Inspire our souls, in all that we do.
For in its beauty, we find our delight,
Umiam Lake shines day and night.

68. Cherry Blossom

In Shillong huge trekky hills,
Where nature's happiness spills,
Lies a festival, pure and bright,
Underneath the cherry blossom's light.
In autumn's tender embrace they bloom,
Cherry blossoms, a fragrant plume,
Painting skies with hues of pink,
As if nature stopped to think.
Amidst the breeze, they softly sway,
In Meghalaya's enchanting display,
Whispering secrets to the breeze,
Dancing under the pine trees.
Festive laughter fills the air,
As people gather, hearts laid bare,
Celebrating nature's fleeting grace,
In this sacred, timeless space.
Ode to the cherry blossoms fair,
In Meghalaya's homely care,
A festival of love and light,
All around the city the blossoms' flight.
So let us join this intriguing scene,
Where dreams and reality convene,
Lovely people and music so dear,
And cherry blossoms bloom everywhere.

69. Enchanting River Gomati

Mata Tripura Sundari,
Bestowed the cosmic seed;
Which unfolded itself into the river,
Catching the full speed.
Running through the hills and valleys,
Piercing through the solid rock;
For many many centuries,
Quenching the thirst of the flock.

For many generations,
It lent a helping hand,
To the soldiers and bubagra (KING)
To protect the Tipraland,

The ethereal beauty of Gomati,
Is enchanting down the hill;
The consciousness of Tripura Sundari,
Is giving the admirer a thrill.

Pray and protect and love,
To keep her in pure form;
Fold your hand to the river,
Chanting the blissful aum.

70. The Feeble and the Bold

Everyone come out of sorrow,
Powerful and disdain;
All the tears will be gone
Fading away the pain.
Life is busy all the time,
In endless parade of daily chores;
All the living is awaiting death,
In the mourning waves of the sinking shores.
Everything is transient,
You me and this beautiful world;
Everyone is transient,
The feeble and the bold.
Forget and forgive your dear ones,
Embrace them and let it go;
Nurture your relationship,
And do away with your ego.
Accept the ebbs and flaws,
Of ever-changing world;
Enter the oblivion,
Oh! feeble and the bold.

71. Embrace Equity

In the worldly desert,
She is the fertile oasis,
A propounder of life,
Protector and fortified glacis;
Yet she is subjected to suffering,
Subdued with maleficent force,
Exploited, deprived and deplored,
Tagged the underserved coarse.
Let's work hand in hand
To bring a positive vibe;
Embolden, galvanize and cheer,
The untrodden women tribe.
We got to be just with them
Provide equal opportune,
Too much of patriarchy;
Now be the companion boon.

We choose to rise together,
We held hand with integrity;
Be a part of the movement,
Commit and embrace the equity (Theme of IWD 2023).
Strike the #EmbraceEquity pose_IWD 2023
Poem composed to celebrate International Women's Day_2023 on the request of Archana E.

72. Living in Fear

Skilled man and a lovely family,
He had seven kids;
He had amassed fortune,
To meet all their needs.
Lovely wife and a giggling home,
Wonderful family's epitome;
Had a niche for everything,
And a perfect upbringing.
Then comes the social turbulence,
People on killing spree;
Societal imbalance,
Giving minor a third degree.
Worried for his kids,
Hid them in the wild for months;
Fearing family's safety,
He could not confront.
He was born in this land,
Living for many century;
Fought for the country's freedom,
Are asked to leave on the contrary.
He is the son of the soil,
He has his part on it;
He has the right to live,
But they deterred his grit.

Authority came to aid,
After two years of pain;
All the property snatched,
Victims are in disdain.
Penniless and hopeless,
He took a refuge now;
Nine life shattered,
Lost his quality endow.
Enough of suffering and pain,
Stop the hatred and fear;
Let us all live in peace,
Make all your judgement clear.

73. Keep Moving

Keep moving forward,
Even if you don't see the light;
There is a definite dawn,
Even after the darkest night.
Keep moving forward,
Till you hear the siren,
Of merciless death
Approaching towards you
From the holy island.
Move towards your goal,
Beating all rejection;
Leave behind despirited,
Surpassing all dejection.
You can then look back,
From the peak of the world;
Laggards laggin by,
Your winning colours unfurled.

74. To Make You Always Smile

I have to fall down from my heights at times,
I have to compromise with my soul;
For you my love at times,
I have to compromise with my goal.
I owe all my achievements to you,
All I have today is yours;
You are with me today,
Opened are all the doors.
All I do today is for you
All your dreams are mine;
All your sorrow and pain,
Shivers up my spine.
I promise to do the best,
To make you always smile;
I will ensure my libido high,
To keep you productive and fertile.

75. Be a True Son

Son to Father

You are no more cool,
Grey haired and half bald;
My circle and my gathering,
Your presence is uncalled.
Your clothes are withered,
And you carry too much weight;
Fed up with your presence,
And your careless distrait.

Your bleary eyes,
You are over the hill;
Lack of enthusiasm,
And nothing more to thrill.
You being a father,
Never cared for me;
Never met my demands,
Never let me free.
Stay away from me,
Let me live my way;
Don't be my barrier dad,
Don't add to my dismay.

Mother to son

Kind patient and loving,
He is the anchor;
Holding the family together,
He saved us from all canker.
He has seen all odds,
To see you rise above;
All he expects from us,
Is a little care and love.
Selfless, unpraised and unnoticed,
The epitome of sacrifice;
He has lived for us,
Gladly given up his paradise.
Despite your rudeness,
His love is undettered;
His commitment for the family,
Is unconditional and unheard.
He still toil for you,
In the scorching sun;
For your happiness dear,
He never had a fun
Though you are grown up,
He is still undone;
Have pride in him,
Be a true son.

76. The Highway to the Goal

The highway to the goal
Is the lonely one;
Painful difficult journey,
You got to walk along.
No one walks with you,
Till your reach your goal;
When the destination is reached,
Follows you the entire world.
Set your dream and persue,
To cross the difficult terrain;
Make your mind up,
To endure the stress and pain.
There will be mental exhaustion,
And you would want to quit;
Always remember not to,
Give up your goal and submit.
Winners are the ones,
Who can resists all odds;
And can hold the thunder,
And the lightening rods.

77. Judge Me No More

Your subtle looks tell me,
That you everyday do;
Judge no more my love,
I am human like you.

The graceful days are gone,
Future looms in the dark;
Things will come Back to life,
Said the passing by lark.

I need your strength and care,
I need your positive word;
Anymore debate on this,
Would be silly and absurd.

Weighty silence filled night,
And the distress soul;
Want to voice it's pain,
Before the death takes its toll.

Stop pointing the flaws,
Look at my beautiful soul;
Tears almost on the edge,
I am toiling it hard to hold.

Don't point fingers at others,
Introspect your degraded soul;
Change your perplexed thought,
For mystery of life to unfold.

Make a move of your own,
Mind your graceful life;
Take a positive step,
Join hands with others to strive.

78. Daughter Natalie

Far away in the country side,
There was a man;
He had a happy family,
Beautiful wife and daughter Natalie.
Their life was quintessence and full of joy,
Natalie was happy with her wooden toy;
Rapacious society had a toll on their life,
So he left his little kid with his wife;
He began his journey to material gain,
He had only goal simple and plain;
Carrying in his heart a mixed pain,
He traveled to the distant land.
He wanted to accumulate money and gold,
His desire for wealth was uncontrolled;
For his family he earned all riches,
Expensive shirts and flattering britches;
Haven't however seen them for decade,
That gives him a heart break.
One fine day a news came,
He is no more his friend exclaimed;
Even the last goodbye, he couldn't say,
For them it felt like a doomsday.
When his body was turned to ashes,
All the wealthy dreams shattered,

His soul was then called to heaven;
And was asked a petty question,
How many days did you live your life,
With your family, your kid and your wife;
His soul then said, pardon me oh Lord,
Worldly material and a life deplored
This question in the world was never heard of,
His vision was blurry and his sense distort;
My vision of happiness was off beam,
Was carried away by the worldy dream;
Never lived a day in harmony,
And disappointed my Natalie.

79. The Biggest Disgrace

The happening character passed away,
His story remained untold,
I tried to awaken the departed soul
In order for the story to unfold.
The soul began his story,
That was hidden beyond the horizon,
Human beings are the only one,
Who annihilate the environ.
The frightening cloud And the thunder said,
The intelligent and the civilised race,
They are the biggest disgrace,
To the mother earth and it's resources.
Arriving out of the clear blue sky,
Uncalled apocalypse of human race,
Leading to the end of the road,
Chaos and destruction with no grace.
I prophesied you with conviction,
It is high time for their eviction;
To protect mother nature and other race,
From the blunder of smartest disgrace.
Don't not trust them, they are insane;
They are bad in all their campaign,
Cruel and gruesome with their ill design ,
They'll leave the beautiful earth malign.

80. Lived an Imprudent Life

All the worldy gains,
And the money I made;
Left me dying in pain,
Did not come to aid.
All I took with me
When I reached the heaven,
Was the tainted soul,
And all the sins seven.
The Lord staring at me,
Asked me buy back your soul;
With all your power and might,
And your treasure and gold.
I put a relentless effort,
In acquiring all the riches;
I live in worldy pleasure,
Topped the rating of fitches(financial rating agency).
Lived in the faked dreams,
Lived an imprudent life;
Ignored the awakening sound,
Coming from the heavenly fife.
Oh! Lord forgive me,
Give me the ruthless pain;
For loosing the humanity,
For the worldy gain.

81. The Poet and the Sea

The vast and forlorn sea,
Expanding to eternity;
Looking for a poet to share,
It's pain of immortality.
Poets come and go;
Have composed for ages beside me;
It's tearing me apart,
The life of eternity.
I want to be mortal,
Mortal like the men;
I want to leave this earth,
And want to be born again.
I am dying a painful death,
For almost infinity;
It is awful to exist
Being the immortal sea.

82. A Swarm of Gyre

I had a complete life
And then my girl left me;
Life took a you turn
And misfortune possessed me.
I was still okay
As I was with my good friends;
Living a newly acquired life,
Catching up with the new trends.
Throughout the day and night,
I am at the mountain high;
Nothing mattered to me,
Without wings I can fly.
I have the stuff with me,
Which is sweet and gaudy,
Sinking deep into to it,
I care for nobody.
The days passed by,
I sunk fully into it;
Now it's not just a stuff,
It became by breath.
Now fully into this hell
I am destined to doom;
Please take me out of it,
I want to live and bloom.

This is not the place,
Where I wanted to be;
Give me another life,
Forgive me oh! Thee.
Stay away from this
Say no to the first syringe;
This is hell for you,
I am now convinced.
Live your wonderful life,
Stay away from this fire,
This is not a glitter,
It's a swarm of gyre.

83. You Overlooked My Lucidity

You have always been complimented,
But you overlooked my lucidity;
I have been snubbed away,
By your unethical rigidity
I awaited my whole life,
Though it was a moment short lived;
You broke my trust,
And am dejected and deceived.
Admiration stands good,
When it comes from both the extremity;
Otherwise in the association,
It bring unheard anonymity.
Let's stay interconnected,
With quintessence life;
With the smile and glory
And do away with the rife.

84. Let Go of Your Ego

Let go of your behaviour,
Let go of your ego;
Mingle with the being
And control your libido.
There are things,
Bigger down the road;
Relax for a while
Keep aside your work load
Get out of the abstract ideas,
And drill down to reality;
Love being yourself
And cherish your actuality.
Turn off your gadgets,
And introspect your own realm;
Connect to your consciousness,
Under the shadow of elm.
Learn to live your life,
Free from the worldly pain;
Pursuit this day in and out,
Your life will easily sustain.

85. Better in the Wilderness

The civilized glory and human achievement,
The aspects of life and it's nothingness;
Human prowess and it's goal
The vacuum and it's emptiness.
The state of being alienated
The traumatic loneliness;
Baseless spirituality,
And the sanctimonious holiness.
Their unfounded lessons,
And their glossiness;
The apostles of religion
And their deceitful godliness.
I am better in the wilderness,
Showering in the fountain;
Let me live my life,
Let me chase the mountain.

86. Own Reasons to Sojourn

Why do you want me to inherit your cult,
Why do you want me to enforce and imbibe;
Understand, the world has changed,
Different sets of goals and out of the box vibe.
You have nurtured me for years,
You have seen me laugh and grow;
Don't try to cover my emotions
With the nasty and cold blow.
I am your progeny, give me freedom to pull through;
Realise the fact, I live with ever changing crew.
I have own reasons to sojourn,
In this transient world;
Let me exist at my behest,
Till my deepest fantasies are blest.

87. Laziness

I'll ruin you, I am not worth a dime
Keep me at distance I may strike you anytime;
I am laziness, leave me little at a time,
Before the dusk covers the sunshine.
Indolence and laxity are by partners in crime,
Trust me oh dear,
I am not worth a dime
I am not worth a dime
You don't deserve to be like this,
I am an evil;
I will ruin your beautiful life;
Like a growling devil.
Don't let me step in,
I will pierce like a ruthless knife;
You will end your youthful days;
Full of resentment and strife.

88. Serene Atmosphere

With all the commotion and urgency,
And the confused state of mind;
The unorganised routine,
And the chaos of the city I left behind;
Now I live in peace,
The ambience is calm and serene;
A small wooden cottage,
The well ordered passerine.
In the calmness of the evening,
You can hear a drop of dime;
What else do you want,
For your peace of mind.
I want to stay in peace
I want to live here forever;
Join me sometimes oh! dear,
To enjoy the serenity together.

89. The Kingdom of Depression

Behind the shadow of all gliteratti,
Biggie dinosaurs and bloodsucking coati
Life is fighting a painless death;
Many beautiful lives took their last breath;
How long will you pain them, oh! dear shibboleth
They are human too and are equally deareth.
Day full of struggle, face full of black soot
Give them equal opportune, let them set their foot,
Depression, anxiety is heading them to doom.
Let them show their skills
We want to see them bloom
Stop paining them, let them take a sigh;
Their dreams are massive you know,
Struggles mountain high.
Guide them to their goal
Be their pole star;
Rinse your tainted soul,
End this bloody cold war.
They need your expertise,hold their hand for a while;
They have the determination to cross the patchy mile.
See them smile and cheer,
At the end of the race;

You also cheer for their win,
And congratulate them on success.
Dedicated to #SSR

90. Filthy Atmosphere

I don't want to show up the street I swear,
Nasty people and a filthy atmosphere;
I hear in silences some call me crumpets,
Unwelcome behaviour and whistles unwanted;
We are humans and we have feelings too,
This sort of treatment will surely make us shrew.
Oh! Dear trust me, I notice all the odd,
It gives me numbness and I vow to ask God!
Is this your creation?
If so, you really need to reshape the next generation.
Show us some respect and give us our space,
Be known for good deeds,
Don't be a reason for our distress.
You've been sculpted beautifully, a wonderful creation of nature;
Damsel is for you, be good to your portraiture.

91. A Wise Man

A Wiseman is wise in both pleasure and pain,
A wise man responds at the time of disdain;
With positivity and and with problem solving skill,
His weaponery of reasoning and formidable will
A Wiseman in wise at the crossroads,
He is too good to decipher and decode;
He is humble and patient and can handle rejection;
He stand firm and channelise his dejection.
To me he is a man in true spirit,
Love and compassion is what he does inherit;
He is the one we can rely in the hour of need;
You can bank on him and comfort yourself indeed.

92. Undisturbed Rest in Peace

You left us in the sharpest turn of life,
We were still too young to live and strive;
When I was young you were my super hero,
Strong character looked fabulous in your woodish sombrero.
Your smile and your gentle nature,
Made you the most loved creature;
I know you are not here anymore,
You'll not return as you've latched the door.
I have lot of things to say concealed deep inside my heart,
They'll never be uttered now as these words fell apart;
You taught me to never give up and to persevere;
I realised now, how I was timid and obscure.
You instilled the sense of care,
You instilled the humour in me;
I promise to carry these traits,
And pass it on as legacy.
If you'd have been here
I would've made you proud;
As you have left us too early,
To live in the abode of cloud;
I'll ever be connected to you,
As long as the universe exists;
Dad may your eternal soul,
Undisturbed rest in peace.

93. Adieu

Eyes flutter, gasp with moan;
Nobody to complain, its ailment of own;
Lived, loved and laughed,
With whatever and whomever I had;
Time to unfurl pinion to conclude an adieu,
Desires unfulfilled remains a few;
Heart is content with memories I collected,
Grateful to all individuals to whom I am indebted.
Crack of dawn shimmer's to renew,
Not a bonjour, lieu an Adieu! Adieu! Adieu.
- Samir Pradhan, Siliguri West Bengal

This poem holds a unique place in my heart, composed by my dear friend, Late Samir Pradhan, at my request as he lay on his deathbed. It is the only poem he ever wrote, crafted in those final, fragile moments of life. With remarkable grace, he embraced the end without regret or complaint, meeting death as one would an old friend.

For me, this is the most beautiful poem I have ever read—a testament to a soul at peace, a spirit willing to surrender with wisdom and acceptance that few of us ever truly achieve.

94. I Can Just Do Nothing

I have learned to be good,
And I learned to behave nice;
I am no more aggressive,
And I turned out to be wise

With little contact with the universe
Now I live in my own cyst;
I am no more angry young man,
Cool, calm and conciliate I exist
I am now trained to live,
And I survive in troubled water;
Now I turn my deaf ear,
To all the violence and slaughter
I can just do nothing,
Nothing to change cruel world;
The inner self of me,
Has totally been hurled;
Now I turn a deaf ear,
To all the happenings around me,
I smacked my heart and soul,
To be really new me.

95. I Spend Time in Loneliness

I spend time in loneliness,
And I look at the ceiling;
I stare at the wall,
And I introspect my feeling.
At times I find myself strange,
And I try to conceal my thoughts;
I at times feel suffocated;
Tangled up in the knots.
Counterfeit philosophies,
And the weird ways of life;
Unrhythmic beating of the drums,
And unpleasant pitch of the fife.
Gives us all a terrific time,
And turns the sage into a human malign.

96. Let's Catch Up

Let's catch up this weekend,
It's been quite a while;
We'll walk down the lane,
And stroll a countless mile.
Down the lane we'll chat,
Chat about the lemons of life;
And let's share our pain,
Join hands to together strive.
After the night falls,
We'll walk to the bar;
After two pegs down,
Blissfully strumming the guitar;
We'll intone the songs of life;
And forget the pain and sorrow,
Coz we have to come to the mainstream;
To join the monotone life tomorrow.

97. I Fall Prey to Your Glamour

HE:

I fall prey to your glamour,
I am in love with your charm;
Oh! Hold me dear,
Around your cosy arm.
Your glimpse is so angelic,
Your eyes are so expressive;
You are the style icon,
Your street sense is impressive.
My feelings for you dear,
Makes me a better man;
I am your secret admirer,
I am your biggest fan.
We met in scanty
Hardly spent time of pleasure;
My memory recalls you,
Reminds me of the short lived leisure.

SHE:

I ignored the signs of love,
I did not read your heart;
I realised your love dear,
After the things fell apart.

I wish I could go back,
Back to the same time again;
Oh! it hurts my love,
Now I regret my disdain.
HE:
If you come we can again unite,
The faded light of tenderness
We can again ignite;
The simmering light
Will gleam again above,
We can happily live our life thereof.

98. The Red Teeth of Nature

The sound of the howling wind,
The red teeth of nature
Is about to approach life
With its horrifying furore.
The life that I am living,
Is always at stake;
The rough patch of the world one day,
Will horribly shake.
The iron rods and the bricks
Willl some day befall;
The tremors of the world,
Will lead to humanity appalled.
There will be tornado and hurricane
The iron vegetation will come to rust;
No structure shall remain,
The entire civilization will turn to dust.

99. I Dance in the Rain

The whole world is asleep
And I dance in the rain,
I sweat it out so that I could fain.
The dream can only come true
When you endure the pain,
Of engrossed and gruelling
And long lasting train (training).
I have absolute faith
In the goal I chase,
I commit to succeed
In this arduous rat race.
I'll plan and prepare and present
Altogether new me,
By setting high standard
And following my own decree.
Masses call me fool
They call me insane,
I follow my own decree
And I dance in the rain
And I dance in the rain.

100. Catch 22 Sitch-The Pandemic

The catch 22 sitch in the world now,
Let's come together to withstand,
Join struggle against it
Is the new universal command...
Fight against it
Cannot be undertaken,
Unless the global citizens
Accept it as a unified challenge.
Let's just be humane
And play our part,
Let's all be geared up
And pull our own cart.
Let's defeat the pandemic
With all our might,
To prevent the annihilation
And to resurrect the civilization alright.

101. Veer Gorkha

Veer gorkha helds his head high,
And defends the motherland
Sweet melody of their songs,
Played with their brass band.

Come on sisters and brothers
Cheer them and clap your hand,
Wonderly dressed brave men
Playing their brass band.

Khukuri in their hand,
Rolling to and fro,
Soldiers shake their legs,
Forming a gyro.

Nothing for these braves,
Is bigger than the motherland,
The saviour of the country
Playing their brass band.

The sacrifices they have made,
Cannot be undone,
A small khukuri for them,
Is stronger than machine gun.

A handful of gratitude and respect,
Is what they all deserve,
Their memories should be cherished,
And they should never starve.

Held them in high esteem,
Let us respect them,
They are the real rock stars,
They are the country's gem.

102. A Metro Dream

A country boy and a metro dream
A sea of struggle and the opportunity slim.
Let's give it a try,
Let's give it a chase
Little step at a time
To develop the base.
To sustain is hard
To persevere is tough.
With so much of pessimism around
And the pathway is rough.
I know I'll not give up
And will keep up the chase;
And will come out winner
In this strenuous rat race.
I'll come out victorious
And shall shine with glory;
My success one day,
Will become an inspiring story.

103. Blame Game

Leaders nowadays,
Play the blame game;
They do this for themselves,
They do this for their fame.
Fame for infinity
Is love for humanity;
Need of of the hour for fame
Is not polarization;

My nextdoor neighbors
Who shares love and care;
Now looks suspicious
Now looks at me with despair.
Let us unite again
Let us ignore them;
Let them play their game,
On their road to fame.
You and me despaired,
Why spread hatred;
Let us share some love.
Let us again be fair,
To defeat his blame game.

104. Animal Speaks

I am no intelligent and cannot help,
I cannot bring a change and can only yelp
(short, sharp cry.)
Can you hear the mother earth shriek,
Eroding landscape and the mountains bleak.
The excavation and mining of ore,
Became the humans daily chore.
How long will you ail the earth,
Don't you fear the pure air's dearth?
There are future generations to come,
For their sake please plant a clump
Then the posterity will praise your work,
And that will be your priceless perk.

105. Loop Zero

After centuries of advancement,
The world comes back to loop zero.
Superpower and nuke prowess,
The world comes back to loop zero.
Greed for power, wealth and rank,
The world comes back to loop zero.
I'll treatment of animals,
The world comes back to loop zero.
Racism and discrimination,
The world comes back to loop zero.
Hindu, Muslim, Jews and Christians,
The world comes back to loop zero.
Atra Mors, SARS, MERS, COVID,
The world came back to loop zero.
(Atra Mors refers to the black death of the 12th century).

106. Humming Like a Bee

Expressive behaviour of my suppressed emotions,
Exhibit a handful of consciousness,
My desires rest in the rock bottom,
Longing now with seriousness
To erupt violently to the shore.
I fear, I fear it will break out
And the world may again deplore.
Cooperate with the emotion,
It is loner like a sea,
Make peace with the heart again,
It is humming like a bee.
Call me your pal once again,
I need you I am in my knee,
Make peace with the heart again,
It is humming like a bee.
It is humming like a bee.

107. Just a Myth

How am I wearing, and how do I look,
Am I gentle or am I crook.
Oh lord please tell me this,
Am I compassionate or do I piss,
Oh! dear you bear a beautiful genome,
But you suffer from spotlight syndrome.
Give a damn to what people think of you,
So that you give your life a hue
Spotlight syndrome is just a myth,
I m now in the company of high sons of pith
Spotlight syndrome is just a myth,
Spotlight syndrome is just a myth.

Reflections On Northeast India: A Journey Of Discovery

As we reach the end of Echoes of the Northeast, we hope this collection has offered you a glimpse into the unique beauty and culture of this remarkable region. Through these poems, we have aimed to showcase the landscapes, traditions, and stories that define Northeast India—a place often overlooked by those from the mainland.

Northeast India is home to a diverse mix of tribal and non-tribal communities, each contributing to a rich cultural landscape shaped by history and shared experiences. The interplay of these groups enriches the traditions that have been passed down through generations, creating a vibrant heritage that deserves to be celebrated and understood. Here, every hill, river, and valley holds a story, and every festival brings together the joys and sorrows of its people.

We invite you to explore this region further, to taste its delicious cuisine, and to meet its warm-hearted people. The poems in this collection reflect only a small part of the depth and richness found in Northeast India. We hope they inspire you to seek out your own connections with this land and its communities, to witness the enduring traditions that continue to thrive today.

May the echoes of Northeast India resonate in your heart, sparking curiosity and appreciation for its diverse cultures and timeless stories. This book is a bridge to a world that is waiting to be discovered, and we hope it encourages you to embark on your own journey of exploration.

Biography

Krishna Acharya

Krishna is an acclaimed poet whose work delves into the depths of human emotion, nature, and the intricacies of everyday life. His poetry has been featured in literary journals earning him recognition for his lyrical style and profound insights into the tribal food, life, culture and folklore.

Krishna discovered his passion for writing at a young age, finding solace and expression in the written word. He pursued a degree in English Literature, where he honed his craft and developed a unique voice that resonates with readers of all backgrounds.

Krishna Acharya

Drawing inspiration from the tranquil surroundings of his hilly village of Ri Bhoi, Meghalaya, Krishna's poetry often reflects the beauty and serenity of nature. His ability to capture the subtleties of the human experience has made him a beloved figure in the literary community.

When he is not writing, Krishna enjoys long walks , playing cricket, and spending time with his family and friends. He is also an avid reader, continually exploring the works of both classic and contemporary poets and loves to read about the diverse tribes and cultures of India.

www.ingramcontent.com/pod-product-compliance
Lightning Source LLC
LaVergne TN
LVHW041220150826
845673LV00001B/460

* 9 7 9 8 8 9 6 1 0 4 3 9 1 *